Buster the Bully

written by
Maisha Oso

illustrated by
Craig Shuttlewood

WELBECK

There once was a fish who would bully and prank,
make fun of – then laugh at – the fish in his tank.
They nicknamed him "Buster." He busted and battered
all things in his path, 'til they toppled and shattered.

He made fun of Missy,
got Tony in trouble.

He rammed Sammy's sandcastle,
left it in rubble.

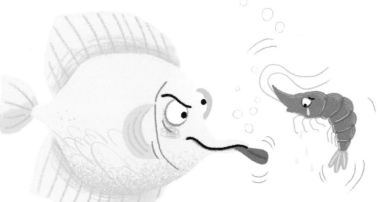

He'd tease Eloise 'til she'd burst into tears

(the same way that **he** did when mocked all those years).

Buster played rough and caused constant commotion.
But the fish said **"ENOUGH!"** and sent him to the ocean.

Buster, unflustered, said, "This is so cool!
Down here there are **millions** of fish I can rule."

"Hey, babies! I'm Buster,
the boss of the sea.
If you're smart little fishies,
you'll listen to me!"

They burst out in laughter
at Buster's remark.
"You can't be the boss ..."

When a shimmering school of sardines passed above,
Buster bust through them to bully and shove.

"... ever heard of a

SHARK?!"

The little fish scattered away in a flash,
as Buster heard something behind him go **splash!**

He turned around quickly and shuddered inside.
"Sweet shellfish! A shark – with its jaws opened

w i d e!"

Buster attempted to cram in a clam, but the clam slammed her shell and then told him to

"SCRAM!"

Then Buster tried hiding behind a large stone, 'til he noticed that stone had two eyes of its own.

Next, Buster tried hitching a ride on an eel,

but was **zapped** in a snap like a microwave meal.

He took cover and hid
in a forest of kelp ...

... when he heard a voice bawling and calling out, **"Help!"**

The littlest fish from his earlier quarrel
was trapped in the tiniest crack in the coral.

The shark heard her shout
and squealed, "Dinner tonight!
Delicious! This fish is
a perfect-sized bite!"

Buster was stunned and appalled by his gall.
"How could a shark pick on someone so small?"

"That fish is in trouble!" So Buster reacted.
He zig-zagged until the big shark was distracted.

The shark took the bait
and ferociously followed,

then Buster dived deep
to avoid being swallowed.

He swam for his life, but the shark was much faster.
He dipped left and dodged right – escaping disaster!

He froze when he felt the shark's nose on his tail.
Then he saw it, and rammed it, and woke up …

...a **WHALE.**

Once the whale saw the shark, dinner plans fell apart,
and Buster's luck changed – right along with his heart.
The shark was sent scurrying. "Save me," he whined,
as he **swished** through the sea with the whale close behind.

This scary encounter helped Buster relate to being the bully *and* being the bait.

Regretting his actions, yet filled with relief,
he swam back to speak to the fish in the reef.

"I'm sorry for shoving. Please pardon my bluster.
I'm changing my ways from today!" exclaimed Buster.

The welcoming crowd chanted, "Buster the Brave!"
But Buster said, "Hey guys, my *real* name is Dave."

Far off, in a voice sounding frightened and frail,
the shark whimpered,

For Selah, Elijah and Judah.
Every day and in every way, be kind. – M.O.

For Ellie & Rory. You amaze me every day. – C.S.

An Upside Down Book

Published in 2021 by Welbeck Children's Books
An Imprint of Welbeck Children's Limited, part of Welbeck Publishing Group.
20 Mortimer Street London W1T 3JW

Text Copyright © 2021 Maisha Oso
Illustration Copyright © 2021 Craig Shuttlewood

Maisha Oso and Craig Shuttlewood have asserted their rights under the Copyright,
Designs and Patents Act, 1988, to be identified as author and illustrator of this work.

ISBN 978-1-80129-009-8

Printed in China
Commissioning Editor: Alli Brydon
Designer: Kathryn Davies

10 9 8 7 6 5 4 3 2 1